The Paperboy

MORNING STAR GAZETTE

LOADING ONLY

MORNING STAR GAZETTE

story and paintings by

Dav Pilkey

Orchard Books   New York

Orchard Books, 95 Madison Avenue, New York, NY 10016

Manufactured in the United States of America. Printed by Barton Press, Inc. Bound by Horowitz/Rae. The text of this book is set in 24 point Times New Roman. The illustrations are acrylics and india ink reproduced in full color.

10 9 8 7 6 5 4 3 2 1

Library of Congress Cataloging-in-Publication Data. Pilkey, Dav, date. The paperboy / story and paintings by Dav Pilkey. p.   cm. "A Richard Jackson book"—Half t.p. Summary: A paperboy and his dog enjoy the quiet of the early morning as they go about their rounds. ISBN 0-531-09506-1. — ISBN 0-531-08856-1 (lib. bdg.) [1. Newspaper carriers—Fiction. 2. Morning—Fiction.]   I. Title. PZ7.P63123Pap   1996   95-30641

MORNING
STAR
GAZETTE

With thanks to Kinney Whitmore

The mornings of the paperboy
are still dark
and they are always cold
even in the summer.

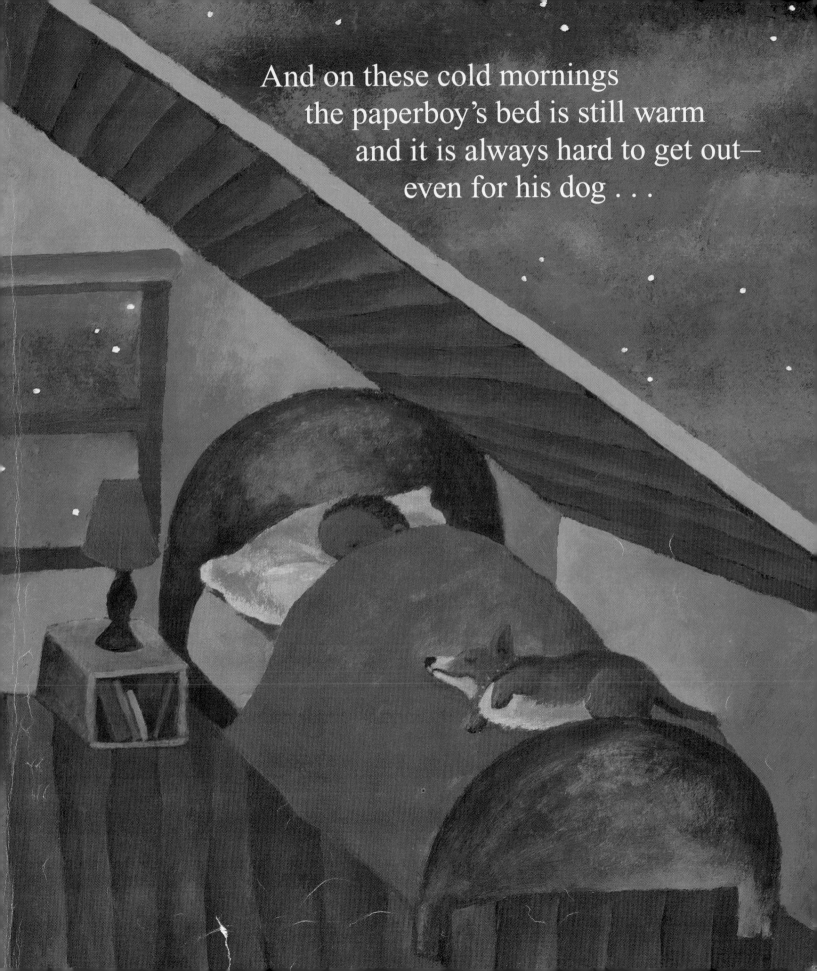

And on these cold mornings
the paperboy's bed is still warm
and it is always hard to get out—
even for his dog . . .

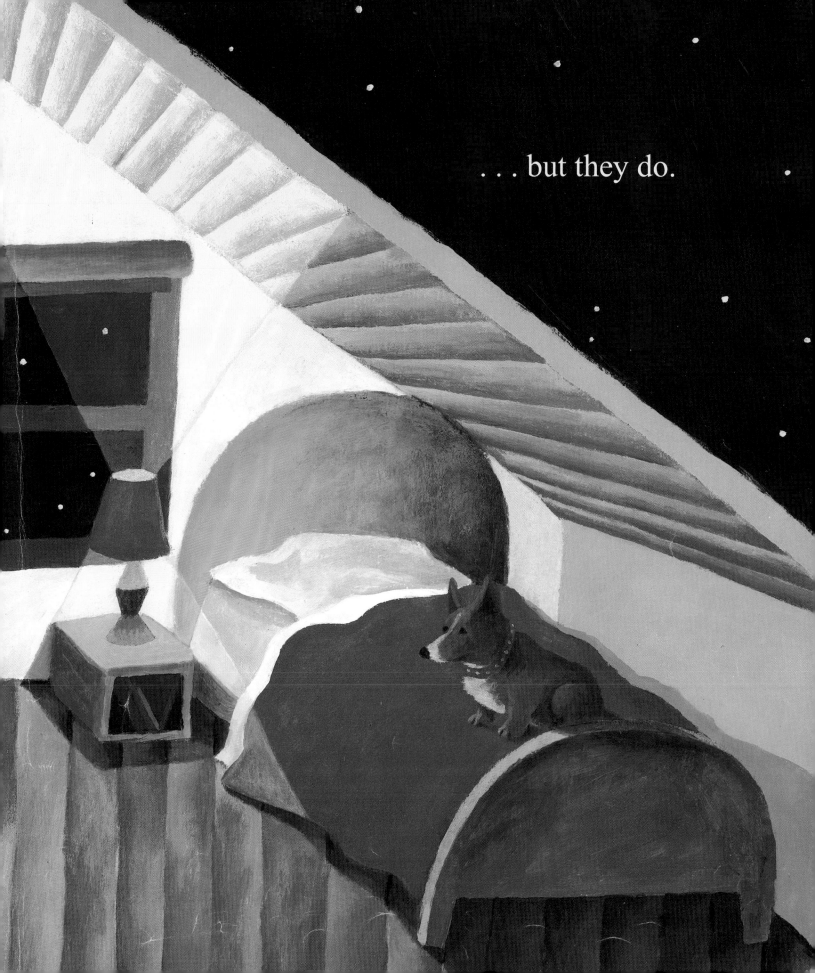

. . . but they do.

And softly they step down
the quiet hall
past the door where the paperboy's
father and mother are sleeping.

Past the door where his sister
is asleep.

And down to the kitchen
where they eat from their bowls.

And out to the garage
where they quickly fold their papers,
snapping on green rubber bands
and placing them in a large red bag.

It's hard to ride a bike
when you are loaded down with newspapers.
But the paperboy has learned how to do this,
and he is good at it.

The paperboy knows his route by heart,
so he doesn't ever think about
which house to pedal to.

Instead, he is thinking about other things.
Big Things.
And small things.
And sometimes he is thinking about
nothing at all.

His dog, too, knows this route by heart.
He knows which trees are for sniffing.
He knows which birdbaths are for drinking,
which squirrels are for chasing, and
which cats are for growling at.

All the world is asleep
except for the paperboy
and his dog.
And this is the time
when they are the happiest.

But little by little
the world around them wakes up.

The stars and the moon fade away
and the skies become orange and pink.

And when the paperboy has delivered
his last newspaper,
he and his dog race home.

And his empty red bag flaps behind him
in the cold morning air.

and his sister is downstairs watching
Saturday morning cartoons.

And back inside his own room
the paperboy pulls down his shade
and crawls back into his bed,
which is still warm.

And while all of the world is waking up,
the paperboy is going back to sleep
and his dog is sleeping, too.
Their work is done . . .

. . . . and now is the time for dreaming.